THE WHITE PONY

a tale of great love by Sandra Byrd

paintings by Sarah Waldron

WATERBROOK
PRESS

THE WHITE PONY
PUBLISHED BY WATERBROOK PRESS
5446 North Academy Boulevard, Suite 200
Colorado Springs, Colorado 80918
A division of Random House, Inc.

ISBN 1-57856-192-2

Published in association with the literary agency of
Janet Kobobel Grant, Books & Such
3093 Maiden Lane, Altadena, CA 91001

Printed in the United States of America
1999—First Edition

10 9 8 7 6 5 4 3 2 1

To Ron and Shirley Gustman
I knew they were Christians by their love.

My people are a gentle tribe. We live in smooth-skinned homes tucked into a dusty part of the land. I, Starlight, have many jobs to do. My brother Turtle and I beat the blankets with heavy sticks. I care for our ponies, but it's not work. It's the best part of my day.

I help my mother pound grain. I don't like that job. I want to hunt and trap horses. It's not fair that Turtle hunts with the men. He thinks he is so old. But I laugh at him. He looks silly with black ash paste on his chubby cheeks. I think his name should be Raccoon.

Even though our work takes many hours, we always save time for fun after the meal. Some nights there is dancing. I laugh and clap as my mother joins the whirling women.

Afterward I lie on a cool patch of grass, gazing at the stars I was named for. Someday my pony and I will ride into the sky and capture one. It could happen. I know this because of the stories.

Story nights are even better than dancing nights. Sometimes the old ones sing. Sometimes they talk about the stories of our people.

Laughing Bird tells the best stories. She has only three teeth, like leftover kernels on an old cob of corn. We must listen closely to hear the words between her whistles and wheezes. Turtle likes the story of how man was made from the dust of the earth. But I always want the story of the white pony. I have asked for it so many times it has become my story. It goes like this.

Ten years after the great rain, the time came for the strongest brave in our village to choose a bride. He did not speak much, but all The People knew he had a large heart. Didn't he spend hours caring tenderly for his ponies, especially his favorite?

Each day the brave silently observed the young women of the tribe. Everyone knew who was the most beautiful girl. Rich braids cascaded down Sunlight's back, shining like a laughing stream without autumn shadows. Her skin was smooth like a stone polished by quick-moving water.

Gray Wolf's daughter Hornet was smart. She taught others to weave plants and threads and to bead pretty patterns. But her name suited her well. Her tongue stung many hearts. Tiny Feathers always knew the best places to scout berries and grub roots. Whoever married her would eat well! But none of these women stirred the young brave's heart.

One day the brave's gaze rested on a young woman working near the others. Forget-Me-Not was plain. She did not weave delicate bracelets of wild daisies or lead others to find food. But he was drawn to her.

Was he touched by the loneliness behind her eyes? Maybe he sensed her aching heart. He, too, wanted someone to walk with in the cool of the evening. He understood and decided to watch her closely.

One afternoon she strolled through the village, cooing to a crying baby. "Ya, ya, ya," she whispered to the baby.

Later, by the fires, the brave again noticed Forget-Me-Not's voice. It was not musical, but when she laughed, he laughed too. He wanted to bring more joy into her life and to share that joy with her.

The brave went to Forget-Me-Not's father. It is the way of The People.

"I would like to take your daughter as my wife," he said. "What will her bride-price be?"

"This one is not beautiful, nor does she know where to find hidden fruit," her father answered. "One pony is enough."

The brave and the father agreed. The young man would come back in seven days to claim his bride.

That night the other girls gossiped. "One pony isn't much," Sunlight said. "My father would ask at least five. But of course, Forget-Me-Not is not a valuable bride."

"It's true," Tiny Feathers chimed in. "My betrothed promised three horses for me!"

Only the brave noticed Forget-Me-Not slipping
away in the shadows, shame welling in her eyes.
He closed the flap of his teepee to think and to sleep.

The next morning he visited the old ones. "What is the biggest bride-price paid in the history of our tribe?" he asked.

They talked and argued for a few minutes. Finally one spoke. "It is said that twenty ponies were paid for Prairie Thorn."

In the days that followed, the brave gathered seventeen of his horses, all but his favorite. In the village he traded fine beaten silver for two ponies, and a pouch of rare shells for one more. When the twenty ponies stood together, he quietly looked them over. Great love filled his heart.

The brave's favorite pony, the one he had raised since birth, stood apart from the others. The brave loved this white pony more than anything else in the world, more than all his belongings combined. The People also admired the brave's pony. Some said it was the finest they had ever seen.

After kissing the pony's coat, the brave led him with the others to the home of his new father-in-law.

The entire village gathered to see. What was the reason for such a sight?

The brave called loudly so all would hear. "Here I am to collect my wife."

The father-in-law shouted, "What is this? We agreed one pony was enough."

"No," said the brave. "My bride is worth more than all others in the history of The People. Here are twenty-one ponies, including my favorite."

Forget-Me-Not walked out of the teepee to join her new husband, her face radiant with joy, her head held high.

For the rest of her life Forget-Me-Not smiled, her eyes and words warm like a spring sun-shower, as she remembered her wedding day. Her husband prized her enough to give up all he had, not because she could offer him anything, but because he loved her.

Now you understand why I, Starlight, always ask for this story. Laughing Bird says it is true, and I know it is. After the stories are over, I run to check on my pony, patting him one last time before bed. I rest my cheek against his flank, loving him and also understanding how much I am loved.

The night is cool, but the tale has warmed me. The story of the white pony is really the story of God's great love for me. Just like the brave, God gave everything He had for us, including His most beloved, Jesus Christ. Why? Because He loves me and wants to be with me forever. That is why I am warm.

I tiptoe home, staring deep into the sky. I whisper, "Thank you."

I know He hears me.

Author's Note

One day I was seeking a novel way to present the gospel story to children when my husband asked what I was working on. When I told him, he remembered an account he'd heard as a boy. Although he didn't remember the details, he recalled a missionary to New Guinea who had compared God's love for us — expressed in the gift of Jesus, His Son — to a bride-price of an extravagant number of pigs. The story moved me.

I changed the pigs to ponies, moved the setting to the early North American plains, and most importantly, added the white pony as a representation of Christ. Then I wove the tale therein.

The New Guinea account may or may not be true, but we do know that the original representation of the church as a bride, with Jesus as her bridegroom, was spoken of by the Lord Himself in Matthew 9, 22, and 25, and by the apostle John in John 3 and Revelation. I hope this allegory helps you cherish the gift of great love given for you.

Sandra